DISCOVERING SHAPES

RECTANGLES

DAVID L. STIENECKER

ART BY RICHARD MACCABE

BENCHMARK BOOKS

MARSHALL CAVENDISH
NEW YORK

Benchmark Books
Marshall Cavendish Corporation
99 White Plains Road
Tarrytown, New York 10591-9001

©Marshall Cavendish Corporation, 1997

Series created by Blackbirch Graphics, Inc.

Printed and bound in the United States.

Library of Congress Cataloging-in-Publication Data

Stienecker, David.
    Rectangles / by David L. Stienecker : art by Richard Maccabe.
         p.   cm. — (Discovering shapes)
    Includes index.
    Summary: Identifies rectangles in the world around us and uses activities, puzzles, and games to explore this shape.
    ISBN 0-7614-0460-0 (lib. bdg.)
    1. Rectangle—Juvenile literature. [1. Rectangle. 2. Shape. 3. Amusements.] I. Maccabe, Richard, ill. II. Title. III. Series.
QA482.S695   1997
793.7'4—dc20
                                96-3172
                                  CIP
                                  AC

Contents

■ ■ ■ ■ ■ ■ ■

It's a Rectangle World

What's a rectangle? Here's a riddle to help just in case you don't remember. See if you can figure it out.

Two lines parallel,

By two lines parallel,

Four corners square.

Put them all together
And see what's there.

OK. So now you remember what rectangles look like. They can be skinny or fat, tall or short, but they all have some things in common—two pairs of parallel lines and four square corners.

4

The world is full of rectangles. How many of these have you seen?

Go on a rectangle search. See how many things you can find in the shape of rectangles. Keep track of what you find in a chart like this one.

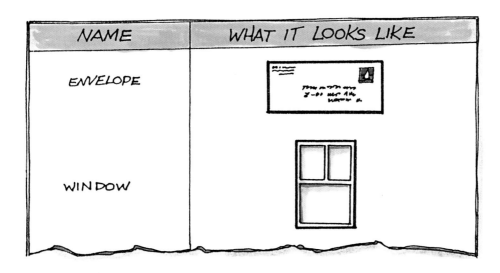

• Have a contest with a friend. See who can find the most things shaped like rectangles.

A Special Kind of Rectangle

Look at this special kind of rectangle. To find out what makes it special, measure each side with a ruler.

4	9	2
3	5	7
8	1	6

A rectangle with all four sides the same length is called a square.

• This square along with its numbers is called a magic square. Add up the numbers in each row and column. Add the numbers in each diagonal. The magic is in the sums. What is it?

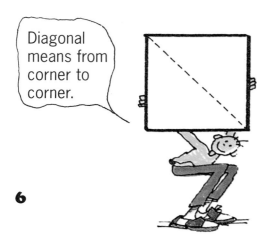

Diagonal means from corner to corner.

• Like other rectangles, squares come in all sizes. How many different-sized squares are in the magic square?

• Now see how many squares you can find in the magic square. Be careful! It's trickier than it looks.

Connect the Dots

Here's a game to play with a friend who knows what rectangles are.

How to play:

1. Make a dot grid like this one. Your grid can be any size.

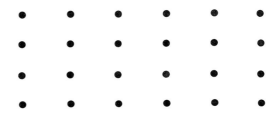

2. Take turns drawing a line between any two dots.

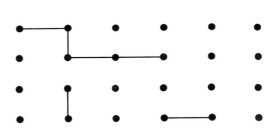

3. When your line makes a rectangle, write your initials in it. Then draw one more line.

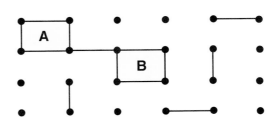

4. The player with the most rectangles wins. Who won this game?

A	A	B	A	B
B	B	B	B	A
B	A	A	A	B

Mosaics from Rectangles

Mosaic is a kind of art in which small colored pieces are put together to make a picture. This section is from a large mosaic mural that was made almost 2,000 years ago. It was made on a wall in the ancient city of Pompeii, Italy. Thousands of pieces were used to make it.

The detail on the left shows one part of the mosaic above. It has been enlarged. Can you tell which part of the mosaic it shows?

See how all the pieces fit together. What shape are most of the pieces?

Make your own mosaics. Use small rectangular pieces (squares work best) cut from construction paper. Use different colors. Paste the pieces onto sheets of construction paper or poster board to make your pictures or designs.

Here is an idea to get you started.

• Make some mosaic pictures or designs to decorate greeting cards and send to friends.

• Use mosaics to make your name or initials to decorate a notebook, scrapbook, journal, or diary.

Rectangle Mazes

In ancient times mazes were part of myths and legends. Today we solve mazes for fun. Here's a maze made out of rectangles. See how long it takes you to get through it. Begin in the center and come out the bottom.

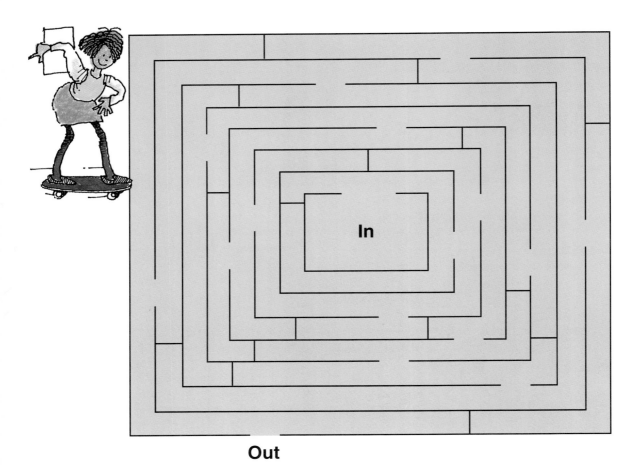

In

Out

• How many rectangles are within rectangles in this maze?

• Try making a maze of your own with a pencil. Begin by drawing rectangles within rectangles. Next decide on the path. Then put in the blockades and use an eraser to make the openings.

Here's a different kind of maze with lots of rectangles. Begin on the green dot at the top of the maze. End with the red dot at the bottom of the maze.

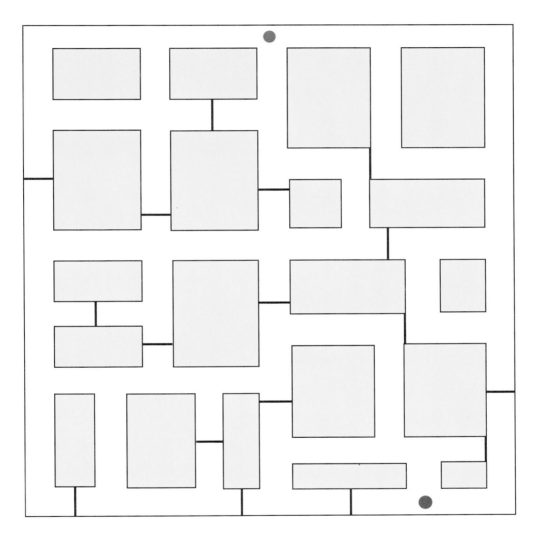

• Which maze was the easiest to solve?

• Now try making a maze like this one. Begin with a pattern of different-sized rectangles. Next decide on the path. Then draw in the blockades.

Toothpick Puzzles

Try your hand at some toothpick puzzles. The first one has been done as an example. Then you're on your own. If things get rough, work with a friend.

Arrange 12 toothpicks like this so they form 4 small squares. Then remove 2 of the toothpicks so that only 2 squares remain.

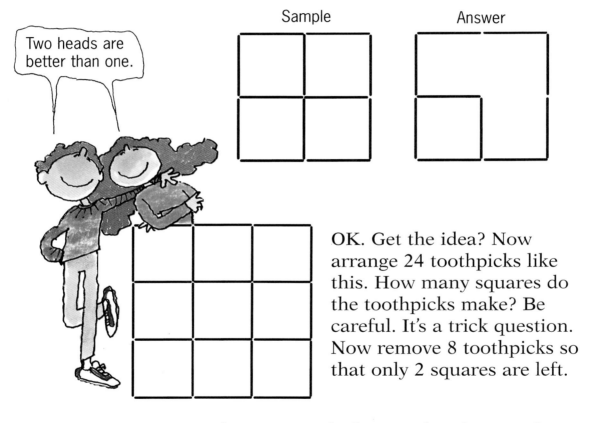

Sample   Answer

Two heads are better than one.

OK. Get the idea? Now arrange 24 toothpicks like this. How many squares do the toothpicks make? Be careful. It's a trick question. Now remove 8 toothpicks so that only 2 squares are left.

- Use the same grid of 24 toothpicks. But this time remove 8 toothpicks so only 5 squares remain.

- Try it again. But this time remove only 4 toothpicks so 5 squares remain.

Now that you're all warmed up, give these puzzles a try. They are a little bit harder. Here's a clue: Don't get the words "move" and "remove" mixed up.

There are two solutions to the problem.

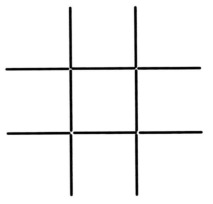

• Make this spiral from 24 toothpicks. Then move 4 toothpicks to make 3 squares.

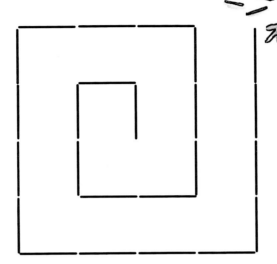

• Now make this grid from 12 toothpicks. Then move 4 toothpicks to make 3 squares that are the same size. There are 3 ways of solving this puzzle.

Use the same grid, but only move 3 toothpicks to make 3 squares that are the same size.

Rectangle Picture Prints

Here's a way to get creative with rectangles. You will need poster paints, paper, small boxes, pie tins, and newspaper.

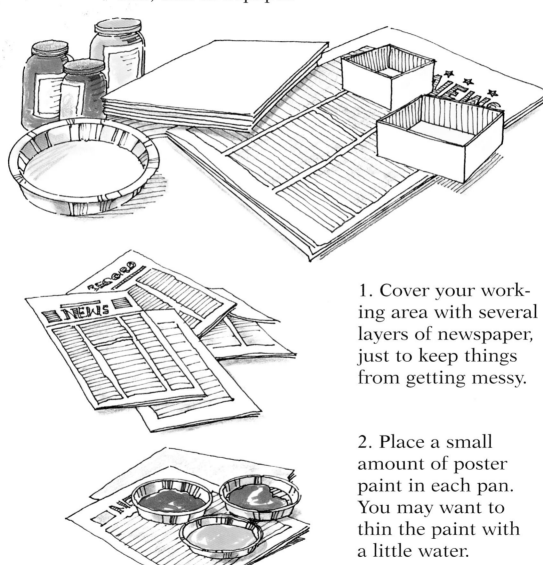

1. Cover your working area with several layers of newspaper, just to keep things from getting messy.

2. Place a small amount of poster paint in each pan. You may want to thin the paint with a little water.

3. Dip one end of a box into one of the poster paints.

4. Press the end of the box onto the poster board. When you lift it up, you should see a colored rectangle. The color may not be even, but that makes it more interesting.

Continue to add rectangles to your picture until it's just the way you want it.

• Be creative. Twist and turn the rectangles. Print them going in different directions. Print one rectangle over another.

• Once you get the hang of it, try making some greeting cards with rectangle picture prints.

Checkerboard Squares

The dotted lines will help you find the answer.

Do you know how may different-sized squares a checkerboard has? Take a look at this checkerboard and see if you can figure it out.

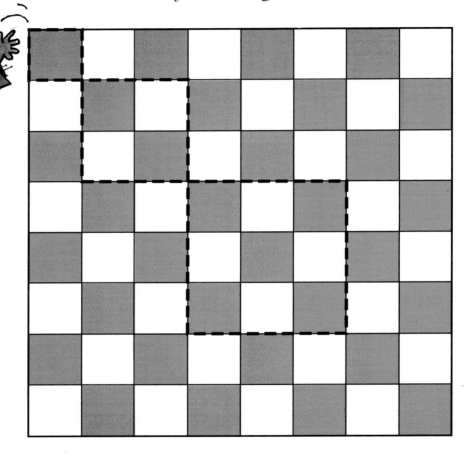

Now consider this: How many squares of different sizes can you find on a checkerboard? That's how many 1x1 squares, how many 2x2 squares, how many 3x3 squares, and so forth.

See if you can figure it out. **Hint:** There are well over a hundred squares in all.

The Fickle Square

Here's a trick that will baffle you and your friends. First get, or make, one inch grid paper. Then draw the lines shown here. Cut the square apart along the lines. You should have five pieces.

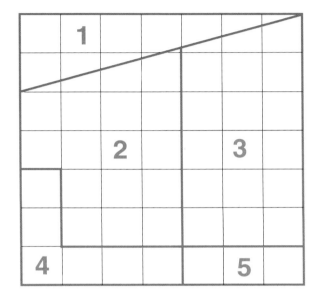

Now put the pieces together like this and see what happens.

There's an extra square in the middle! Put the pieces together the way they were. The square is gone!

Try it several times just to convince yourself. Then show it to your friends. They'll be just as baffled as you.

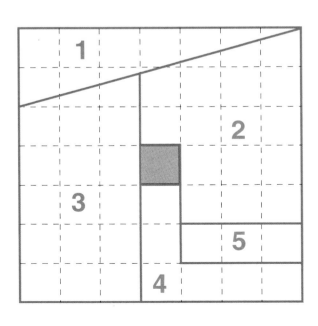

Tangram Rectangles

Almost 4,000 years ago the Chinese made a puzzle by cutting a square into seven pieces. The puzzle is called a tangram. These are the seven tangram puzzle pieces.

• Carefully trace or copy the tangram pieces above onto a sheet of paper. Then cut them out. See if you can fit them together to make a square. You must use all the pieces. It may take a little time, but the rewards are great.

• Now use all the tangram pieces to make a rectangle that is not a square.

• People use tangram pieces to make all sorts of shapes and figures. Experiment for awhile. See what shapes and figures you can make.

The Golden Rectangle

Have you ever thought that you liked the shape of one rectangle better than another? The ancient Greeks believed that one rectangle shape was more pleasing to the eye than others. They called it the Golden Rectangle. Here's how you can make one. You'll need a compass and a ruler.

1. Begin with a square. (Using grid paper may be easier.) Then find the middle of the bottom line. Draw a line from there to the opposite corner.

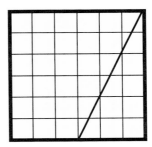

2. Put your compass point on the middle of the bottom line and your pencil on the opposite corner and draw an arc like this.

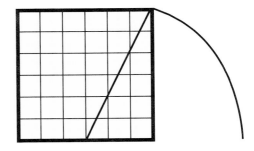

3. Complete your Golden Rectangle by adding these lines to your square. That's it. Is the rectangle pleasing to your eye?

• Try making other Golden Rectangles with different-sized squares.

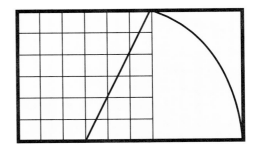

Origami Squares

Origami is the ancient art of paper folding. *Origami* is the Japanese word for folded paper. But it is believed that origami started in China. Try making this origami cup. Begin with a square of paper that is 6 inches on all sides. When you're finished, see if your cup holds water.

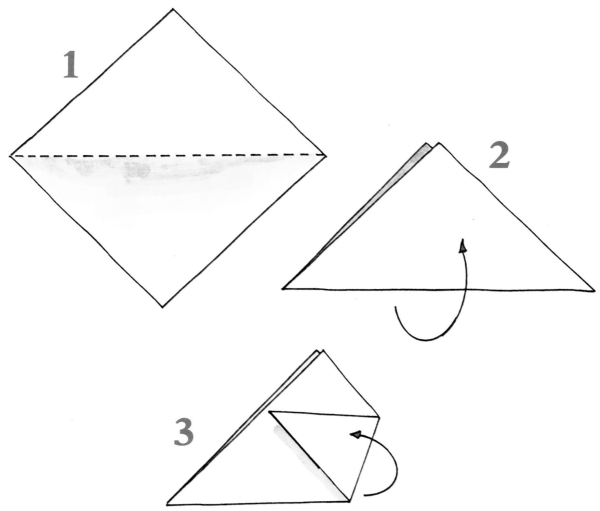

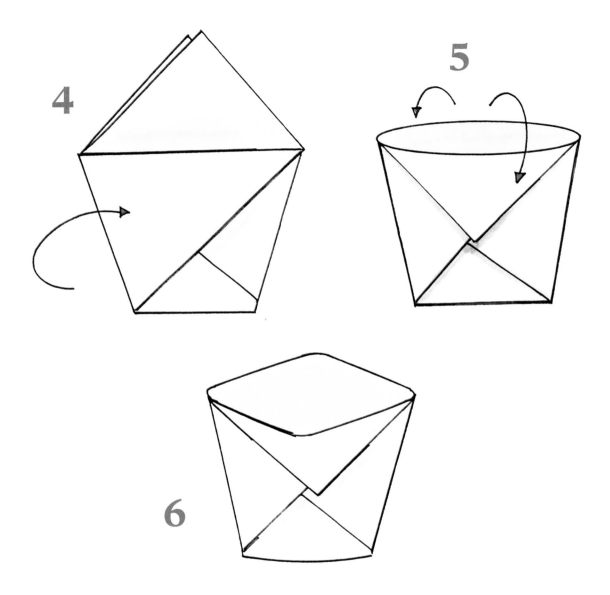

- Make several cups from different-sized squares.

- Decorate your cup with colorful designs, glitter, and by gluing on bits of colored paper.

- Fill origami cups with nuts and candies and give them away as party favors.

Rectangle Puzzles

Try your hand at solving these puzzles. Just follow the instructions.

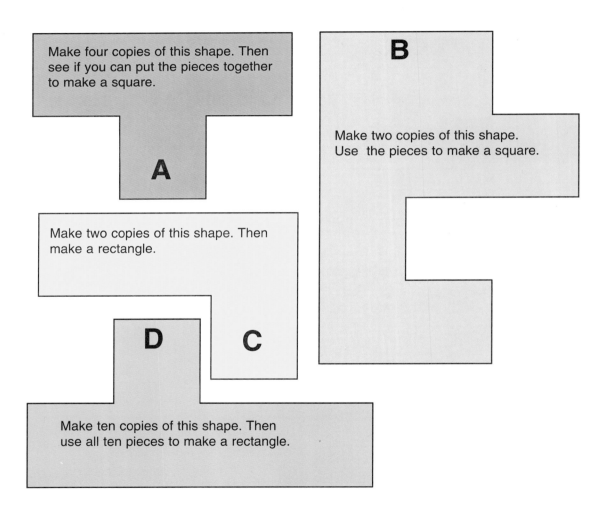

Make four copies of this shape. Then see if you can put the pieces together to make a square.

A

Make two copies of this shape. Use the pieces to make a square.

B

Make two copies of this shape. Then make a rectangle.

D   **C**

Make ten copies of this shape. Then use all ten pieces to make a rectangle.

• Take two A pieces and two D pieces and put them together to make a rectangle.

Rectangle Cards

Here's a way to amuse yourself. You will need twenty-four playing cards. Lay the cards out to make the perimeter of a rectangle. Start like this:

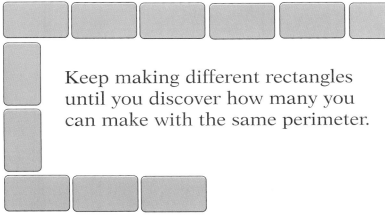

Keep making different rectangles until you discover how many you can make with the same perimeter.

Perimeter is the distance around a shape or figure.

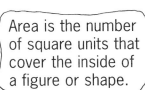

When you are done, try the same thing with different numbers of cards. If you have a really big table, you can try the whole deck!

Now try this. Make twenty-four square cards. Lay the cards out to show the area of a rectangle like this.

Area is the number of square units that cover the inside of a figure or shape.

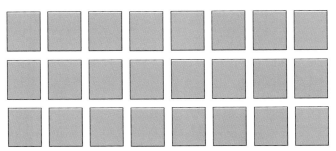

• Discover how many different rectangles you can make with the same area. Then try the same thing with a different number of cards.

23

One-Cut Rectangles

These shapes don't look much like rectangles. But here's what to do to change all that. Copy or trace a shape onto a piece of paper. Then carefully cut it out.

By making one cut somewhere on the shape, you should be able to put the two pieces together to make a rectangle. You can try flipping one of the pieces over. Good luck!

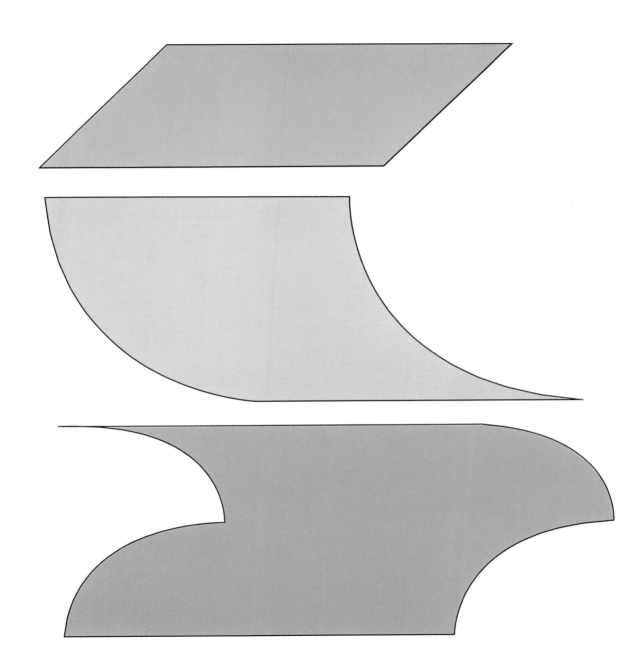

Pentaminoes

Pentaminoes are shapes that you can make with five squares. There are twelve different shapes in all. Here are seven of them.

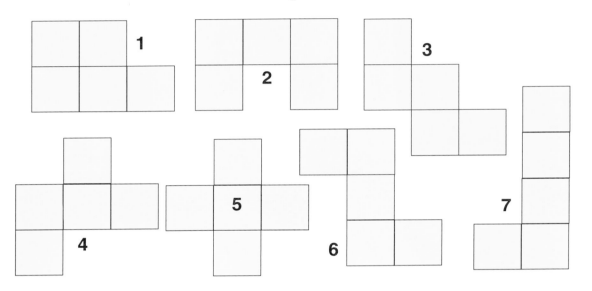

• Make a copy of pentaminoes 1, 2, 4, 5, and 7. (Each square has one-half inch sides.) Then cut them out and arrange them so they fit inside this square.

• Now cut out five squares all the same size. Use them to make the other five pentamino shapes.

• Draw and cut out the five pentamino shapes you made. Then fit them together to make a square.

Answers

Pps. 10–11, Rectangle Mazes

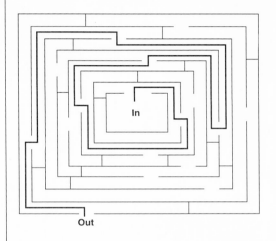

Pps. 4–5, It's a Rectangle World
No answers.

P. 6, A Special Kind of Rectangle
The sum of each row, column, and diagonal is 15.

There are 3 different-sized squares in the magic square.

There are 14 different squares in all:

      1x1 squares: 9
      2x2 squares: 4
      3x3 squares: 1
           total: 14

P. 7, Connect the Dots
No answers.

Pps. 8–9, Mosaics from Rectangles
The shapes are mostly rectangles.

There are 7 rectangles within rectangles.

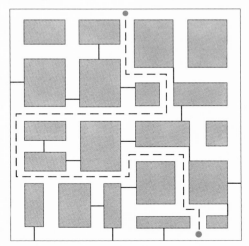

Pps. 12–13, Toothpick Puzzles

The toothpicks make 14 squares in all. You can make these 2 squares by removing 8 toothpicks:

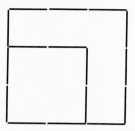

By removing 8 toothpicks you leave these 5 squares:

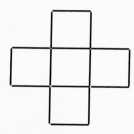

By removing 4 toothpicks you leave these 5 squares:

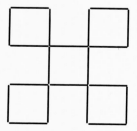

Here are two ways to turn the spiral into 3 squares by moving 4 toothpicks.

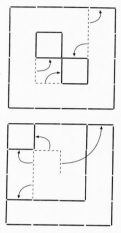

Here's how to move 4 toothpicks to make 3 squares that are the same size.

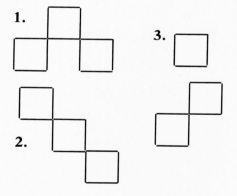

This shape can also be made by moving only 3 toothpicks.

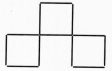

Pps. 14–15, Rectangle Picture Prints
No answers.

P. 16, Checkerboard Squares
There are 8 different-sized squares on a checkerboard.
There are 204 squares in all.:

     1 square that is 8x8
     4 squares that are 7x7
     9 squares that are 6x6
    16 squares that are 5x5
    25 squares that are 4x4
    36 squares that are 3x3
    49 squares that are 2x2
    64 squares that are 1x1

P. 17, The Fickle Square
No answers.

P. 18, Tangram Rectangles

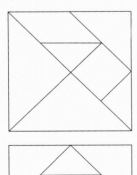

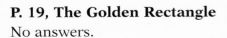

P. 19, The Golden Rectangle
No answers.

Pps. 20–21, Origami Squares
No answers.

P. 22, Rectangle Puzzles

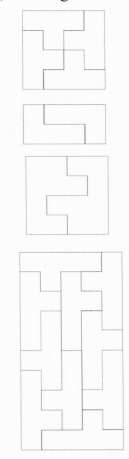

P. 23, Rectangle Cards
You can make 6 rectangles with the same perimeters: Two sides with 1 card and two sides with 11 cards; two sides with 10 cards and two sides with 2 cards; two sides with 9 cards and two sides with 3 cards; two sides with 8 cards and two sides with 4 cards; two sides with 7 cards and two sides with 5 cards; two sides with 6 cards and two sides with 6 cards.

You can make 4 rectangles with the same areas: 1 x 24; 2 x 12; 3 x 8; 4 x 6.

29

Pps. 24–25, One-Cut Rectangles

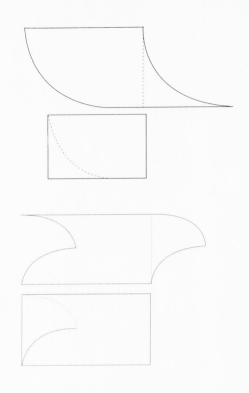

P. 26, Pentaminoes

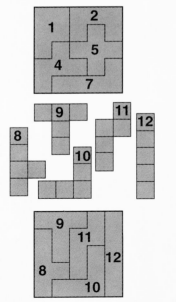

Glossary

arc A part of a circle.

example:

area The number of square units that are needed to cover a surface.

column An up and down arrangement of things.

diagonal A line connecting opposite corners of a shape.

example: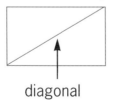

diagonal

grid A pattern of vertical and horizontal lines.

example: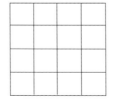

pentaminoes The shapes made by arranging 5 squares into 12 different shapes.

perimeter The distance around a shape.

rectangle A shape with 4 sides and 4 right angles.

example:

row A number of objects arranged in a straight line.

spiral A winding and gradually widening coil.

square A rectangle with all 4 sides the same length.

example: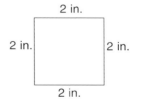

2 in.

2 in.   2 in.

2 in.

tangram A puzzle made by cutting a square into 7 pieces.

Index

Photo Credit:
Page 8: Scala/Art Resource, NY.